The Letter Home

The Letter Home

Timothy Decker

Front Street
Asheville, North Carolina

To my mother and father

Library of Congress Cataloging-in-Publication Data
Decker, Tim.
The letter home / by Tim Decker. — 1st ed.
p. cm.
Summary: A medic sent to the front lines in the trenches
of World War I writes a letter home to his young son.
ISBN 1-932425-50-0 (alk. paper)
[1. War—Fiction. 2. World War, 1914-1918—Fiction.
3. United States Army—Medical personnel—Fiction. 4. Letters—Fiction.] I. Title.
PZ7.D35754Let 2005
[Fic]—dc22
2005014191

The Letter Home

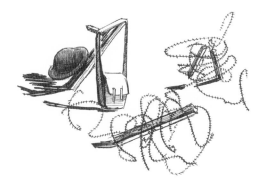

I did not want to write to you until I could say that I would be home soon.

It started with a boat ride.

I'd never seen the sea before, and I saw a lot of it.

And then we walked

through cities,

through fields,

through forests,

then into nothing.

Some nights were alive with fireworks.

Sometimes we played hide and seek.

In school they taught us that this land was flat.

But there are mountains here, built by hand.
They feel higher than the Alps and are harder to climb.

I have seen hundreds of aeroplanes. There are days
when they seem to litter the sky like leaves in autumn.

We must have looked like schoolboys playing in the mud.
But we didn't really play much.

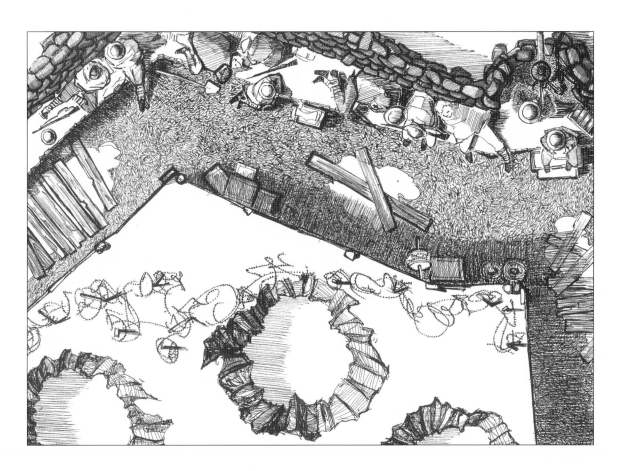

We just read letters, looked at our watches, slept when we could
for as long as we could with our heads down and our ears open.

The days passed slowly.

The nights passed slowly.

Hendricks found a woman's coat. We all laughed at him.
We said that he must have just arrived from Paris.

He said that it kept him warm.

And then the lieutenant caught one of the signal birds.
All that the small slip of paper said was
It ends, 11:00 a.m. 11/11.

The lieutenant asked us what the weather would
be like at home during the spring.

I said a prayer that I learned from an Oxford man
who was sick and in my care back in '17.

He coughed a lot.

It was an old prayer from far to the east.

Compassion as action to ease the pain of the world.

I will see you soon.